The Riverndish

By:

M. J. Yandle

ARPress
ILLUMINATING IDEAS
EMPOWERING VOICES

ARPress
45 Dan Road Suite 5
Canton MA 02021

Hotline: 1(888) 821-0229
Fax: 1(508) 545-7580

Ordering Information:

Quantity sales. Special discounts are available on quantity purchases by corporations, associations, and others. For details, contact the publisher at the address above.

Printed in the United States of America.

ISBN-13:   Paperback   979-8-89356-805-9
                eBook   979-8-89356-806-6
                Hardback   979-8-89356-813-4

Library of Congress Control Number: 2024904236

Growing up I had a creative imagination as most children do. I always had so many unanswered questions, fantasies, wishes and dreams. My life has taken me on many journeys. I have written this book to take you on one and I hope you enjoy the journey as much as I had fun writing it.

Our world is constantly changing. Hug your loved ones often, cherish them and let them know they are loved. Always have hope through uncertain times. Always remember the world can be a better place through the laughter and imagination of children. They are our future, make the best of it for them.

Hopes and dreams are the basis of a children's imagination. Everyone grows up with an idea of who and what they want to be. This book opens up many possibilities that help explain how they become possible.

INTRODUCTION

Past the fourth planet in our solar system and to the right shines one of the brightest stars in the sky. The star is actually a planet mysteriously hidden from view and undiscovered by man, but native to the Riverndish.

The planets name is Valarious and it has been hidden magically from planet earth since the beginning of time. The habitants of the planet, the Valarins, have watched over earth all their life and they have lived for one purpose; to grant every wish for all of mankind. In order to do that, their one goal in life, is to protect and nurture their beloved Riverndish.

VALARIOUS

Valarious is similar to planet earth, with beautiful mountains, oceans, streams, valleys and forests. There's always a cool breeze and the temperature is always pleasant and just right. Food is always abundant and available everywhere on planet Valarious within hands reach.

The Valarins can take any shape, size or form and can travel anywhere through time and space, so no one could ever know what they truly look like. That's how the Valarins can grant every wish and make sure they all come true.

THE RIVERNDISH

Beyond the highest mountains of planet Valarious, through the forest and valleys, in the oceans and streams you will find the most magical creature, the most beautiful fish, called the Riverndish.

The Riverndish is not like a mermaid or merman, but it is similar to a dinosaur or a dragon. The Riverndish can adapt to any body of water all around the planet Valarious and has existed throughout the beginning of time and space.

The tail of the Riverndish is the most beautiful, magnificent, iridescence of light and it glows and shines bright with each motion as the tail moves back and forth flowing gracefully through the water. The colors created by the Riverndish are more beautiful than the colors of a rainbow seen on earth and the waters of Valarious are always glowing with an unlimited pallet of color.

THE GRANTOR OF WISHES

The Riverndish always linger unforgettably in the Valarins' mind until nothing else matters but a wish being granted.

The Riverndish doesn't sleep but it does feed on wishes, dreams and hope. It knows no age, privilege or poverty. It is always listening, waiting to reward only those who truly believe.

Anytime you feel a breeze, or see dandelion seeds blowing past you in the wind on planet earth, the Riverndish has heard wishes, dreams and hopeful thoughts, aiding them all to come true.

If you listen hard enough, you can hear the pleasant chimes from the mystical creature floating atop the wind.

THE JOURNEY

On the planet Valarious, mystical colors are shimmering in the water and just enough light shines through the water only to catch a glimpse of a shimmering tail swimming to and fro, stirring up wishes stored safely in bubbles in the water that float up, up, up to the surface of the water and up into the wind. The bubbles burst in the wind carrying the wishes across streams, valleys, fields, forests, above mountains up into the sky and on into space, continuing on until it reaches its final journey's end.

The wishes never give up and never stop until they reach their final destination. That's why some wishes take longer to come true. It takes time to travel along time and space, and sometimes detours occur along the way.

THE DETOUR

That's what happened to one wish, one very special wish. It got lost along its way to a child on planet earth who only wished for one very special thing. The child's parents had hopes and dreams that this one special wish would come true and encouraged the child to never give up on this wish. The parents gave the child toys and games to try and take the child's mind off the wish, but the child was very determined and wanted this wish more than anything.

On its way to the child the wish ran into a meteor shower in space and was bounced around to and fro until it finally landed on the surface of planet Mars. It lingered on the planet amidst storms and dust particles for days, weeks, even months until one day the dust particles were blown back out into outer space by a huge planetary dust storm and the wish continued on to find the child, however much time had already passed.

THE DESTINATION

The Valarins were keeping track of the wish that the Riverndish had worked so hard to grant, and were doing their best to make sure the wish made it to its proper destination. They knew the child would be much older before the wish could be granted, and there was a possibility that the wish may be forgotten.

By now years had passed. The child was much older now, but the child never forgot about the wish, however, was beginning to have less hope that it would ever come true.

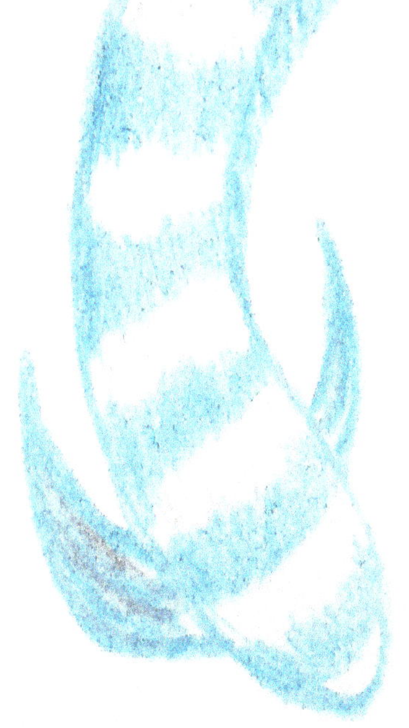

TIME AND SPACE

The wish was tossed about in space bouncing off each star, planetoid and asteroid on its way to planet earth. Then one day it was hit so hard by a particle in space that it was given a huge amount of energy and thrust pushing it closer to earth's orbit.

It raced passed earth's moon and came closer and closer to earth's atmosphere where it was pulled into earth's gravity.

METEOR SHOWER

The wish flew across earth's blue sky like a fire bolt visible to many people on planet earth, then something happened. The wish broke apart into 3 pieces flying across the sky.

It was an amazing spectacle watching the incredible fire balls with flashing tails colored in red, yellow and orange and then disappearing onto land miles and miles away.

LAND FALL

The Valarins had worried that the wish would stay whole and not break apart as planned, but all their hard work had come true. The wish would soon be granted.

The wish found its way to its final destination....

REFLECTION

The child had one special wish but in order to grant the wish, two steps had to be taken before the wish could be granted. The child had wished for a very long time that he would be able to make the most delicious lemon pie, the same that his grandmother made when he was very young. After his grandmother's passing the recipe had disappeared and no matter how hard he tried, he could not replicate the recipe, it was always missing a special ingredient.

The Valarins knew that the first thing they would have to do is figure out what happened to the recipe. After frantically searching the Valarins finally found that the recipe had been put in a special hiding place for the child to find by his grandmother. The second step would be to remind the child where the special hiding place was.

WISH GRANTED

As soon as the wish touched the child's face a kaleidoscope of color filled the room, and as quickly as the color appeared, it disappeared. The child suddenly remembered a hiding place that his grandmother had always placed special items for him and he went running into the living room to his mom and dad yelling "I remember where it's at!"

The child ran outside to the garden shed, flung open the door and ran toward a small wooden box that had been stored there for years. The child opened the box and found the recipe lying on top along with other special items that he had shared with his grandmother while he was growing up. The child ran into the kitchen right away and started carefully mixing all ingredients for the lemon pie making sure no ingredients were left out.

After it was made the child sat down with his parents and they all enjoyed going through all the special items that was in the wooden box while eating a piece of the delicious lemon pie he had worked so hard to make.

INFINITY

The Riverndish and the Valarins were very happy because every time a wish is granted, the planet Valarious is renewed with more energy and magical powers, ensuring that their planet will live on forever through space and time.

THE END

I dedicate this book to my grandma Fern, who I spent most of my childhood with. The best cook I have ever known; she taught me how to laugh, play, cherish my loved ones, and always inspire to be whatever I wanted to be. I hope I can live up to her expectations and make her proud

Hopes and dreams are the basis of a children's imagination. Everyone grows up with an idea of who and what they want to be. This book opens up many possibilities that help explain how they become possible.